Here Come the Easter Rabbids

by Maggie Testa   illustrated by Jim Durk

Simon Spotlight
New York London Toronto Sydney New Delhi

SIMON SPOTLIGHT
An imprint of Simon & Schuster Children's Publishing Division
1230 Avenue of the Americas, New York, New York 10020
© 2016 Ubisoft Entertainment. All rights reserved. Rabbids, Ubisoft, and the Ubisoft logo are trademarks of Ubisoft Entertainment in the U.S. and/or other countries.
This Simon Spotlight paperback edition January 2016
All rights reserved, including the right of reproduction in whole or in part in any form.
SIMON SPOTLIGHT and colophon are registered trademarks of Simon & Schuster, Inc.
For information about special discounts for bulk purchases, please contact Simon & Schuster Special Sales at 1-866-506-1949 or business@simonandschuster.com.
Manufactured in the United States of America 1215 LAK
10 9 8 7 6 5 4 3 2 1
ISBN 978-1-4814-5255-7
ISBN 978-1-4814-5256-4 (eBook)

One bright, sunny Sunday morning in springtime the Rabbids were in a park trying to imitate a yoga class's moves. The Rabbids didn't know what springtime was, and they didn't know what Sunday was (and also, they were not great at yoga). To them this day seemed like any other day.

But it wasn't. It was Easter. The Rabbids certainly didn't know what Easter was . . . but they were about to find out.

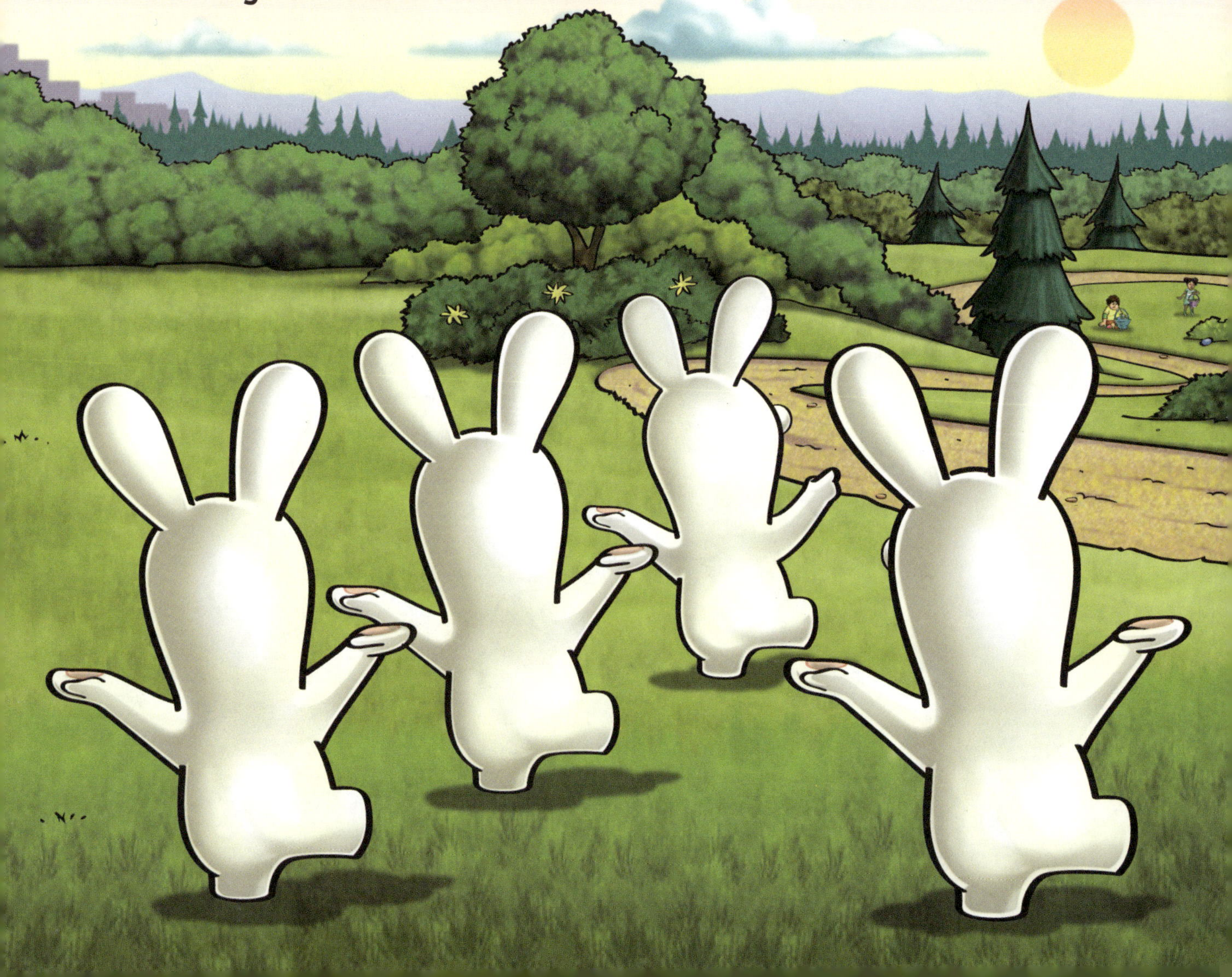

One Rabbid pointed down the hill to a field below. "Bwah?" he said. There were kids everywhere. They seemed to be looking for something. But what?

The Rabbids ran down the hill. They watched as the kids pulled out shiny oval-shaped things from behind tree trunks and under bushes and put them in baskets.

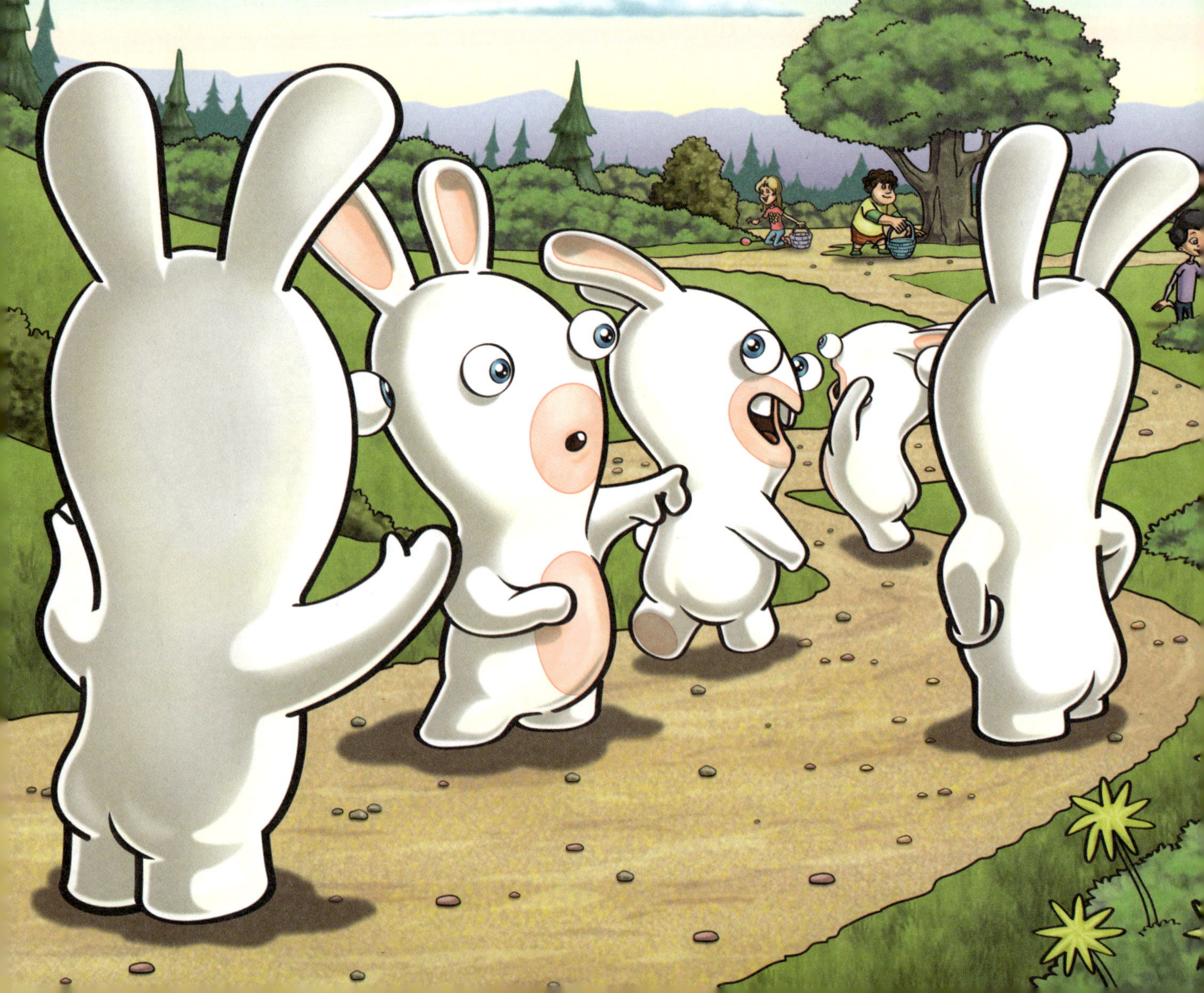

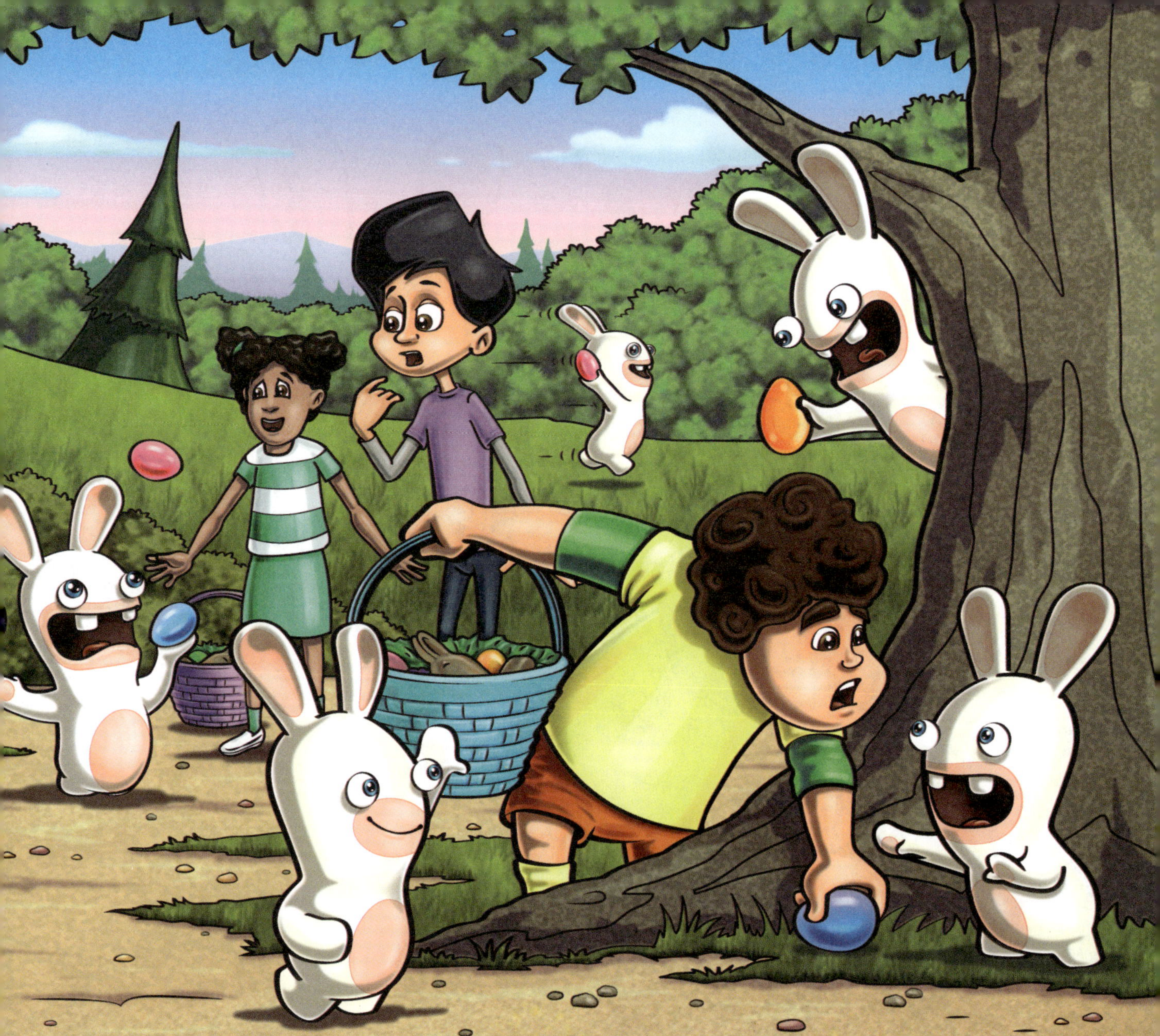

One Rabbid gestured to his friends excitedly. "Bwah, bwah bwah bwah bwah!" he said. The Rabbids could find shiny things and put them in baskets too!

So they went off to do just that. It wasn't long before the Rabbids had found lots of shiny things . . .

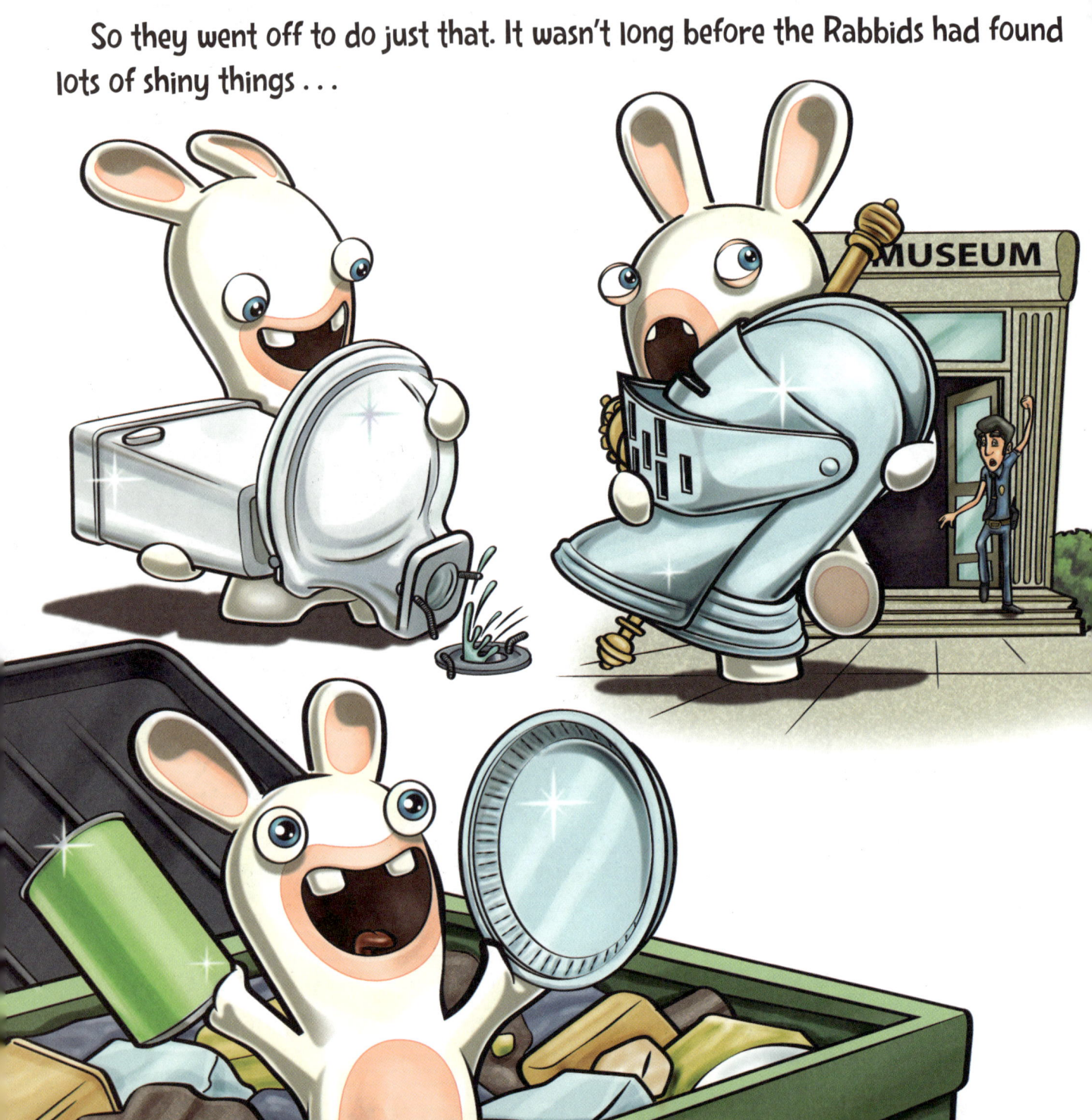

although they weren't exactly the same as the shiny, colorful objects the children had been collecting.

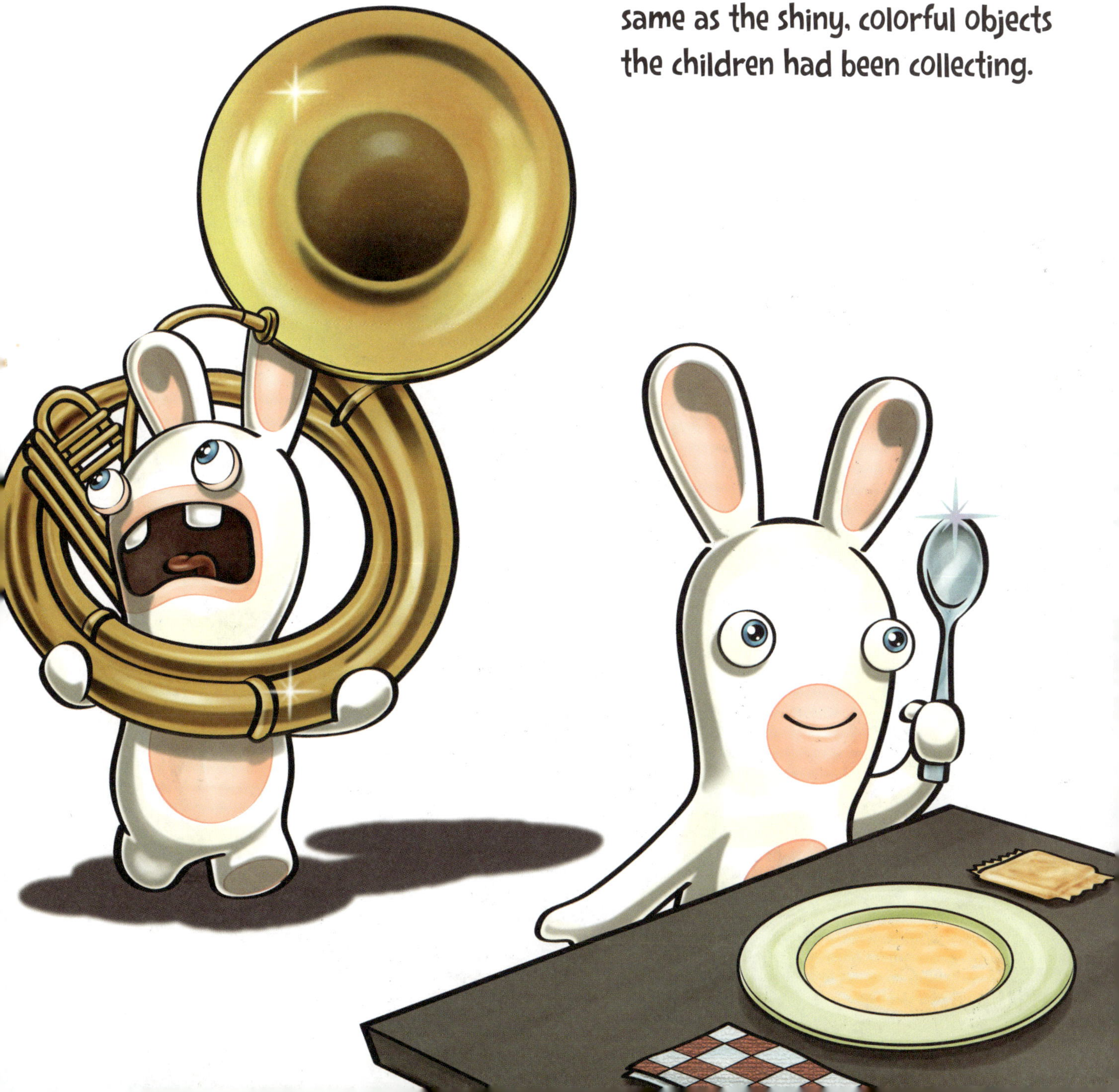

The Rabbids ran back to the field to show off what they had found. They put their shiny objects in the children's baskets, excited to be part of the fun game. But then all the children were upset.

"You're smashing our Easter eggs," one girl screeched.

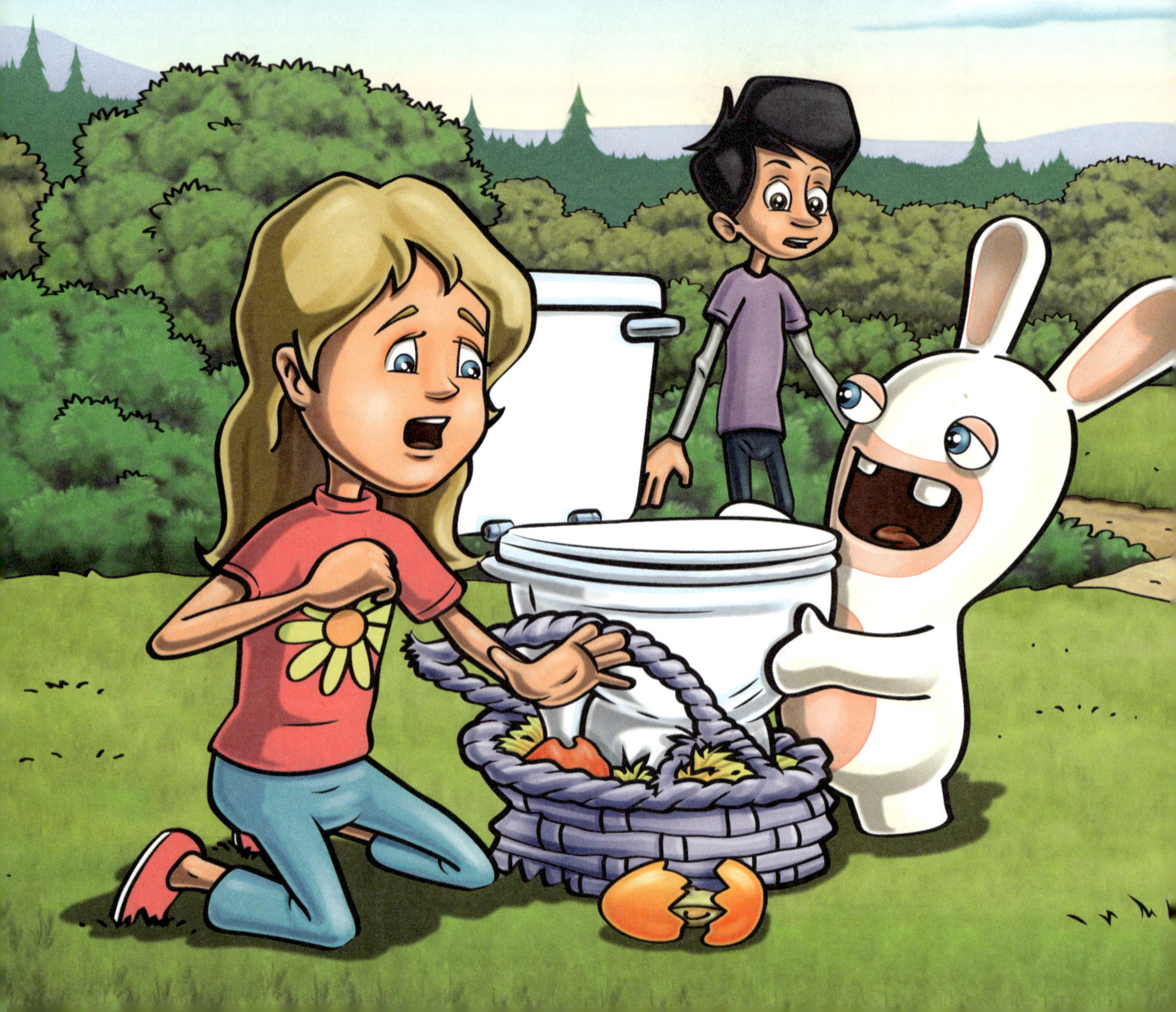

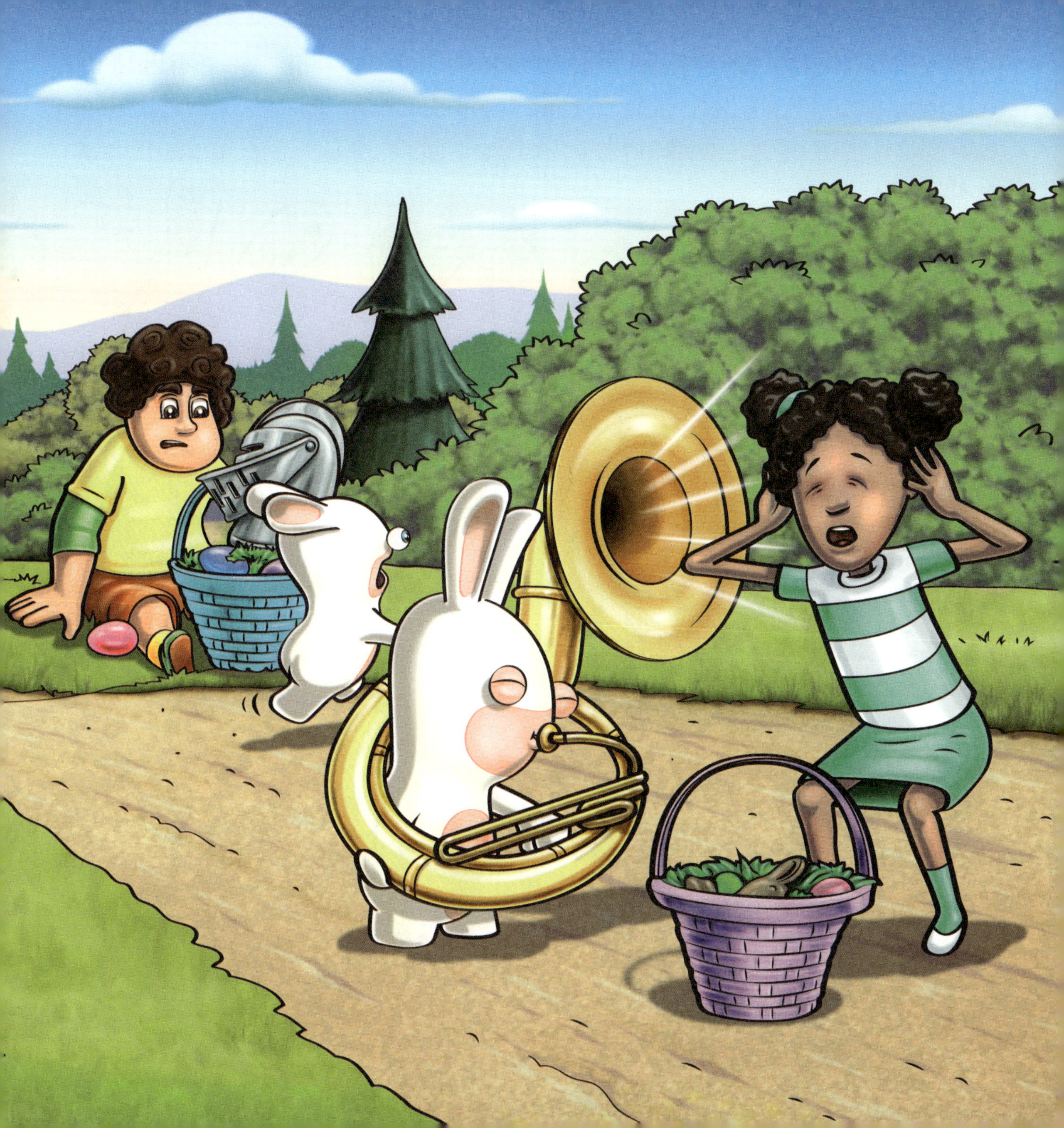

But the Rabbids didn't have time to wonder why the kids were yelling (not that they would have been able to calm them down, anyway). At that moment they saw lots of people walking by. And they were all wearing funny things on their heads.

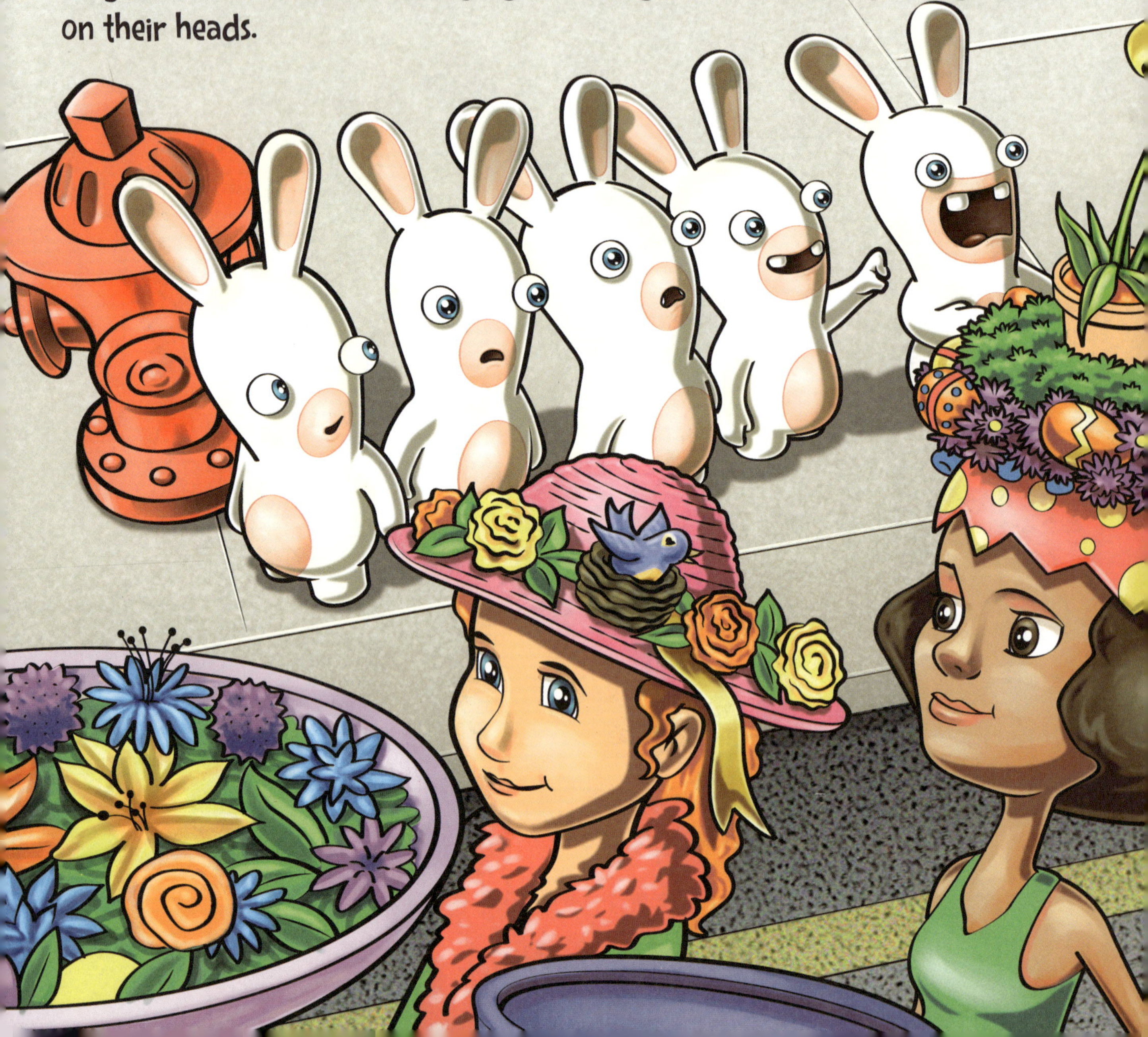

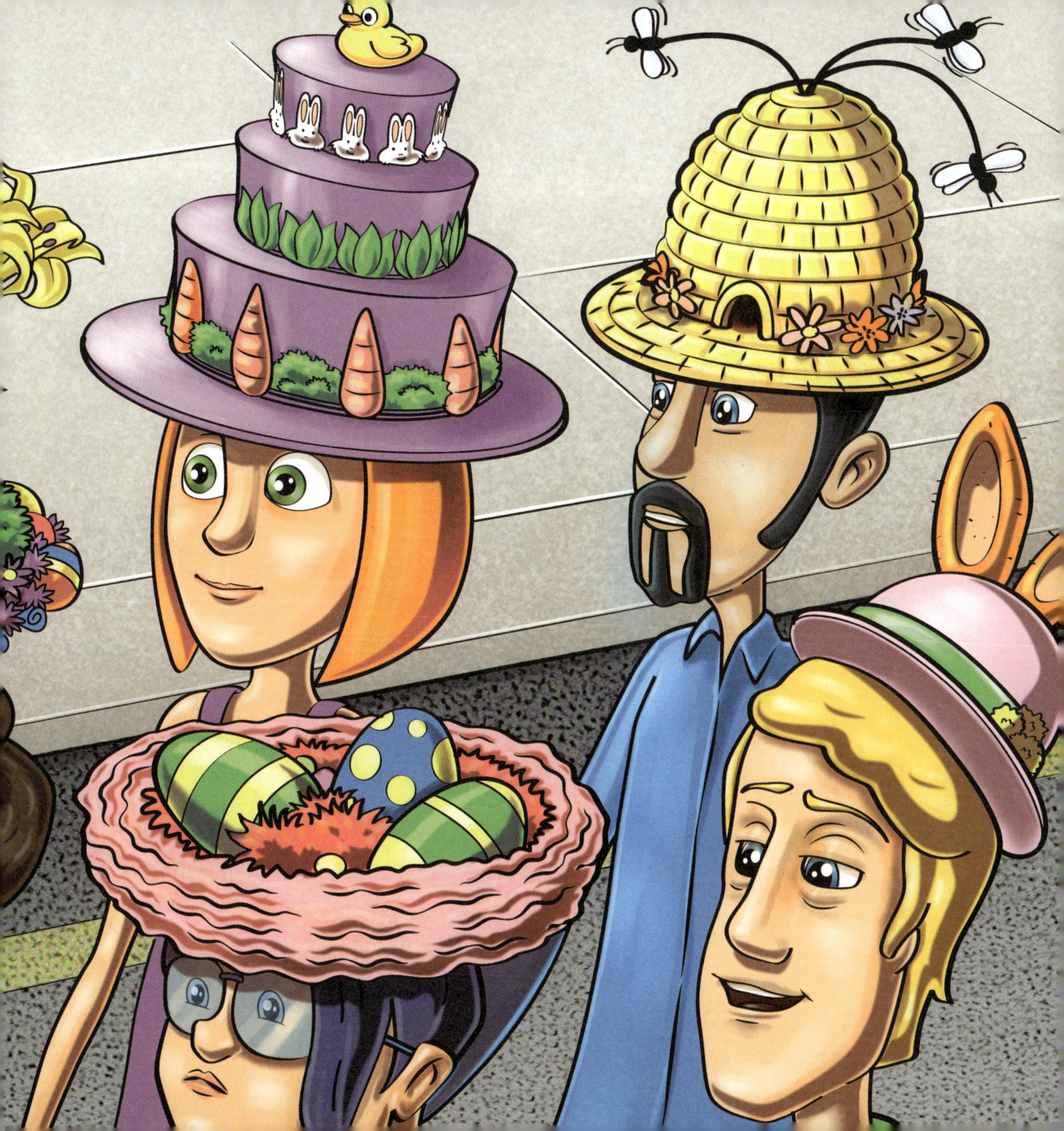

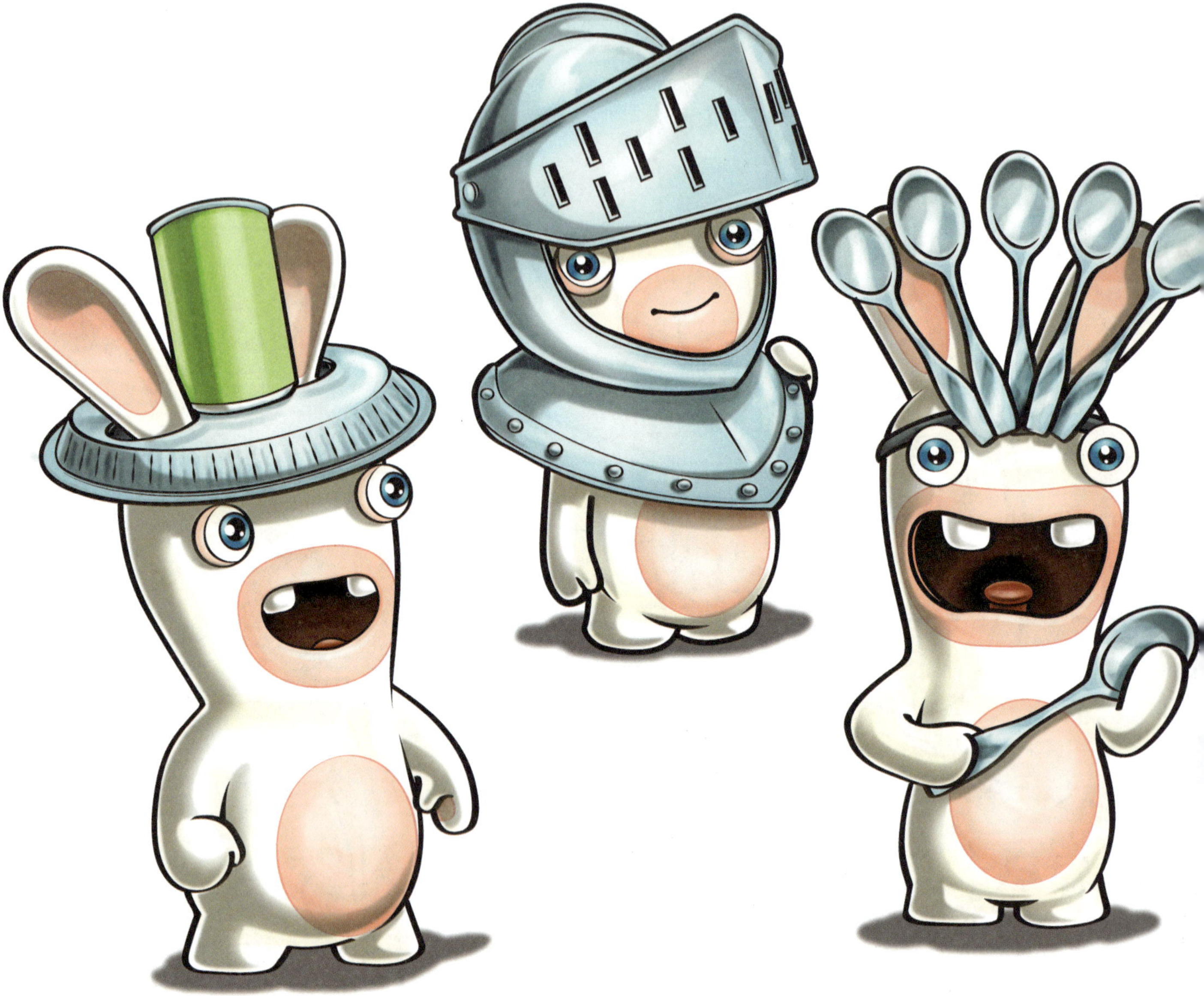

"Bwah, bwah bwah BWAH!" one of the Rabbids said, pointing to the parade that he didn't know was a parade.

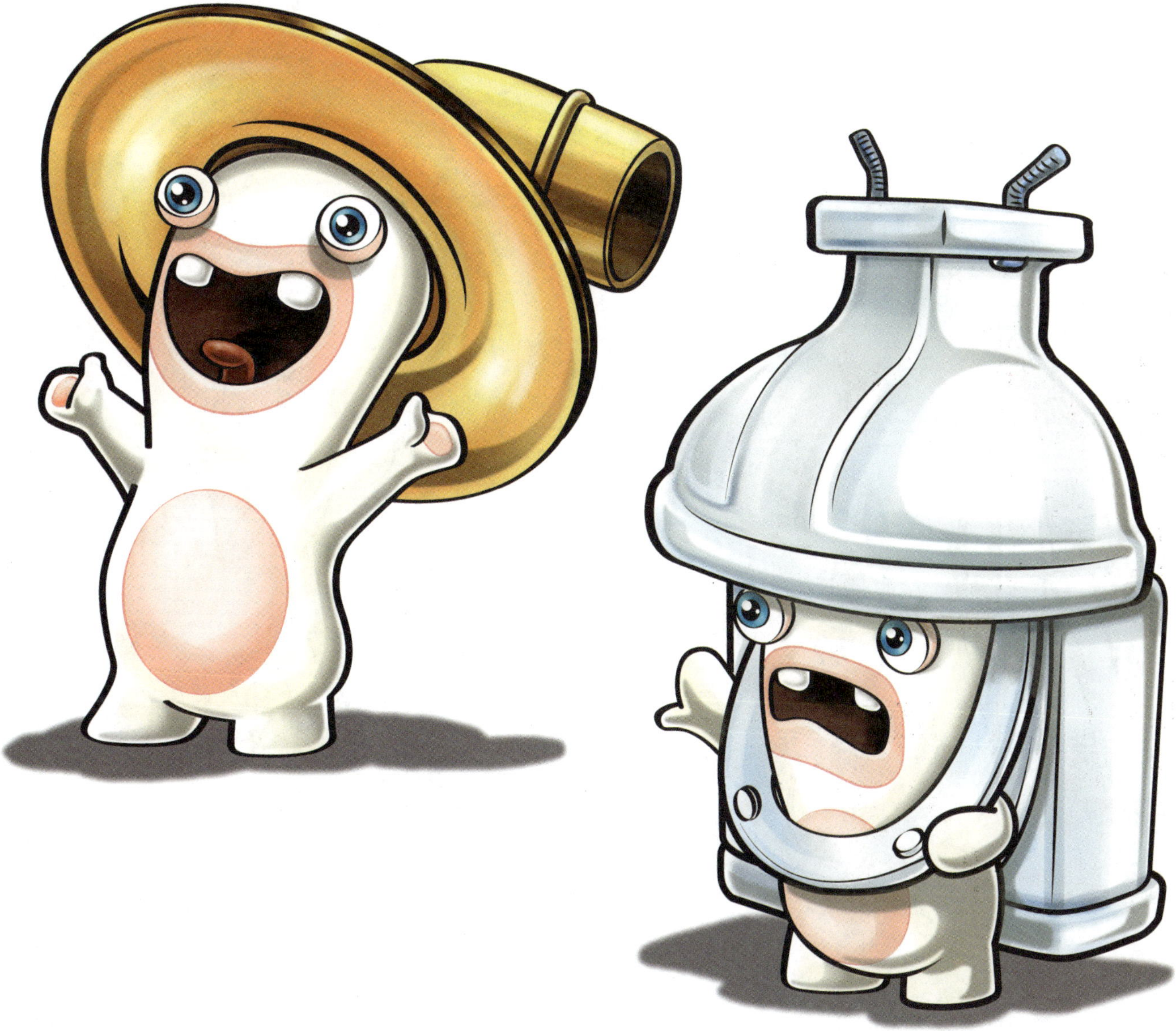

The Rabbids loved to wear funny things on their heads . . . and they had just the things to wear! They hurried off to join the parade.

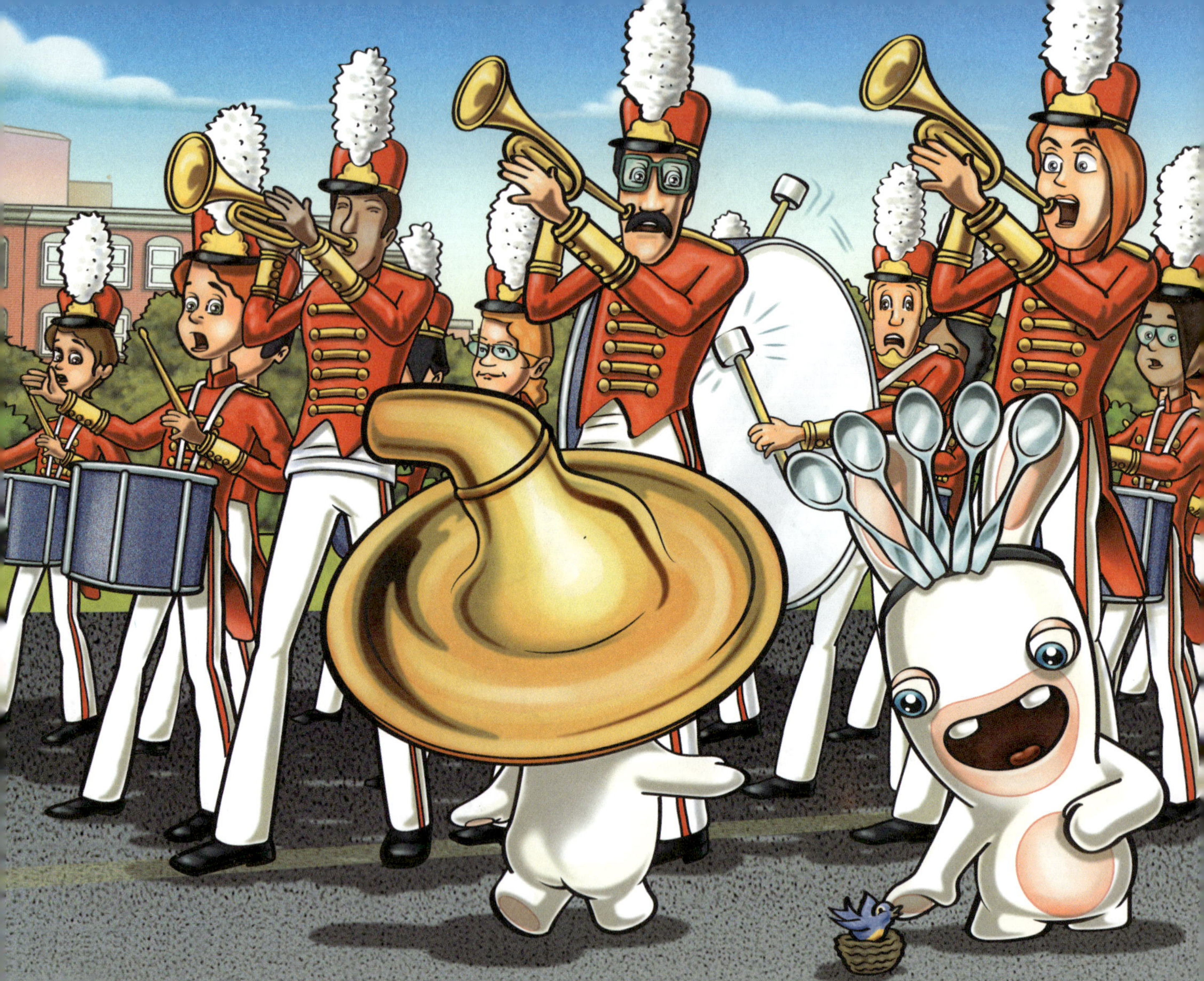

The Rabbids fell into step behind a marching band and began marching in perfect order in the bright sunshine. Of course, they didn't stay like this for long.

"Bwah ha ha ha ha!" cried one of the Rabbids. He had seen something fall off someone's head. The Rabbid ran to put the thing on his own head. That gave the other Rabbids an idea. . . .

"BWAH!" they shouted gleefully as they began taking hats off other people's heads and putting them on their own.

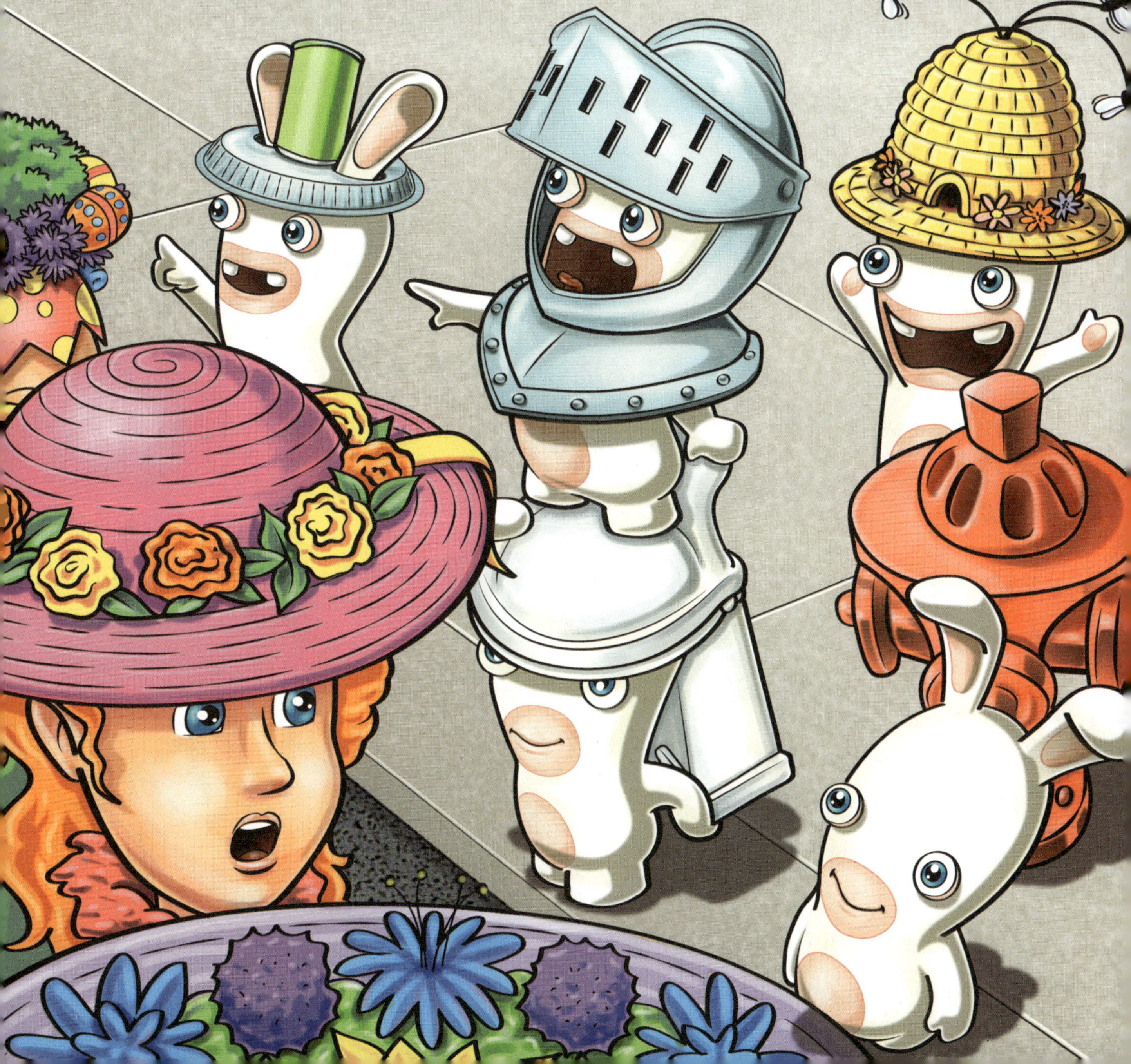

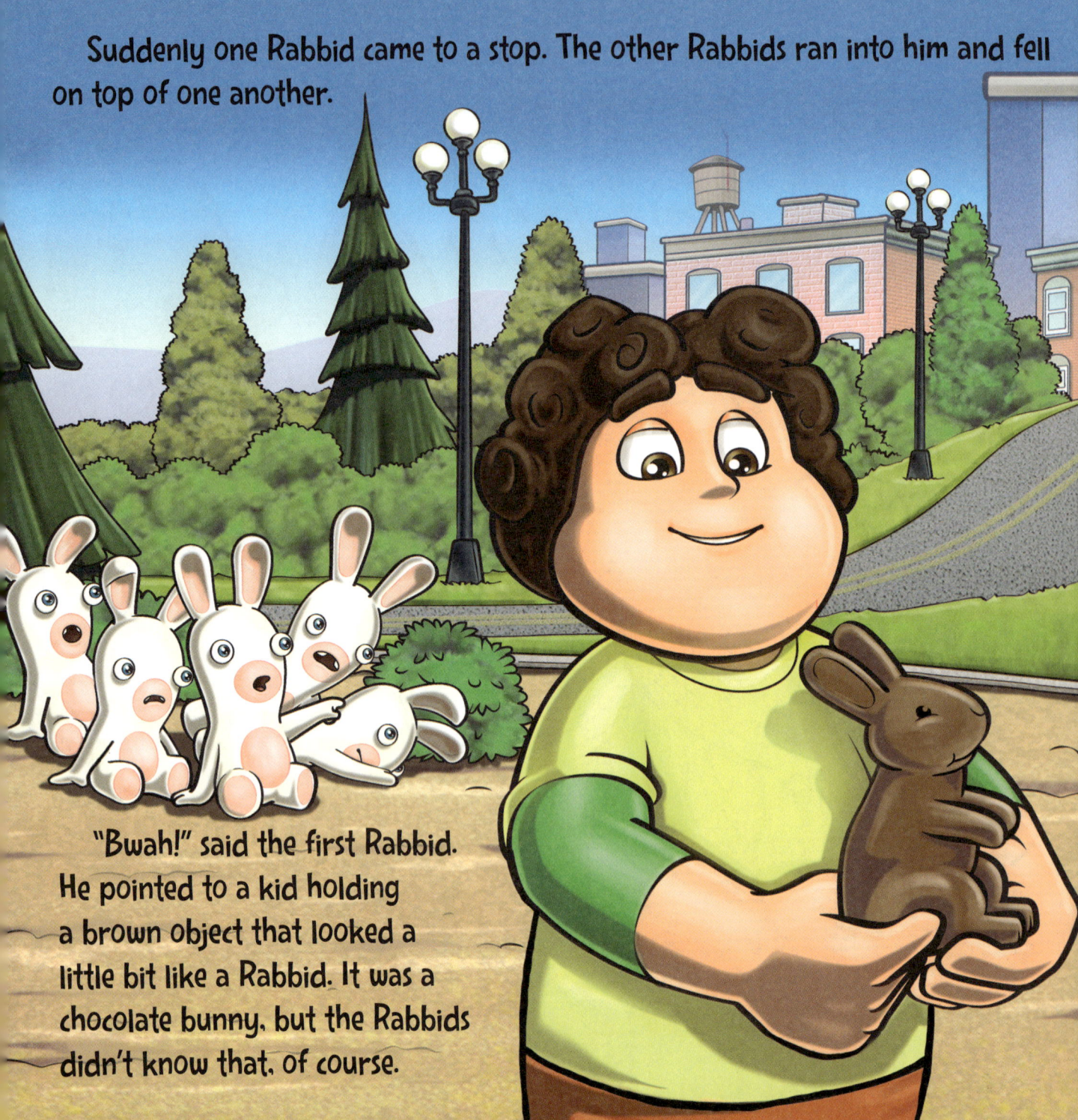

Suddenly one Rabbid came to a stop. The other Rabbids ran into him and fell on top of one another.

"Bwah!" said the first Rabbid. He pointed to a kid holding a brown object that looked a little bit like a Rabbid. It was a chocolate bunny, but the Rabbids didn't know that, of course.

CRUNCH! With one giant bite, the kid ate the head right off the chocolate bunny!

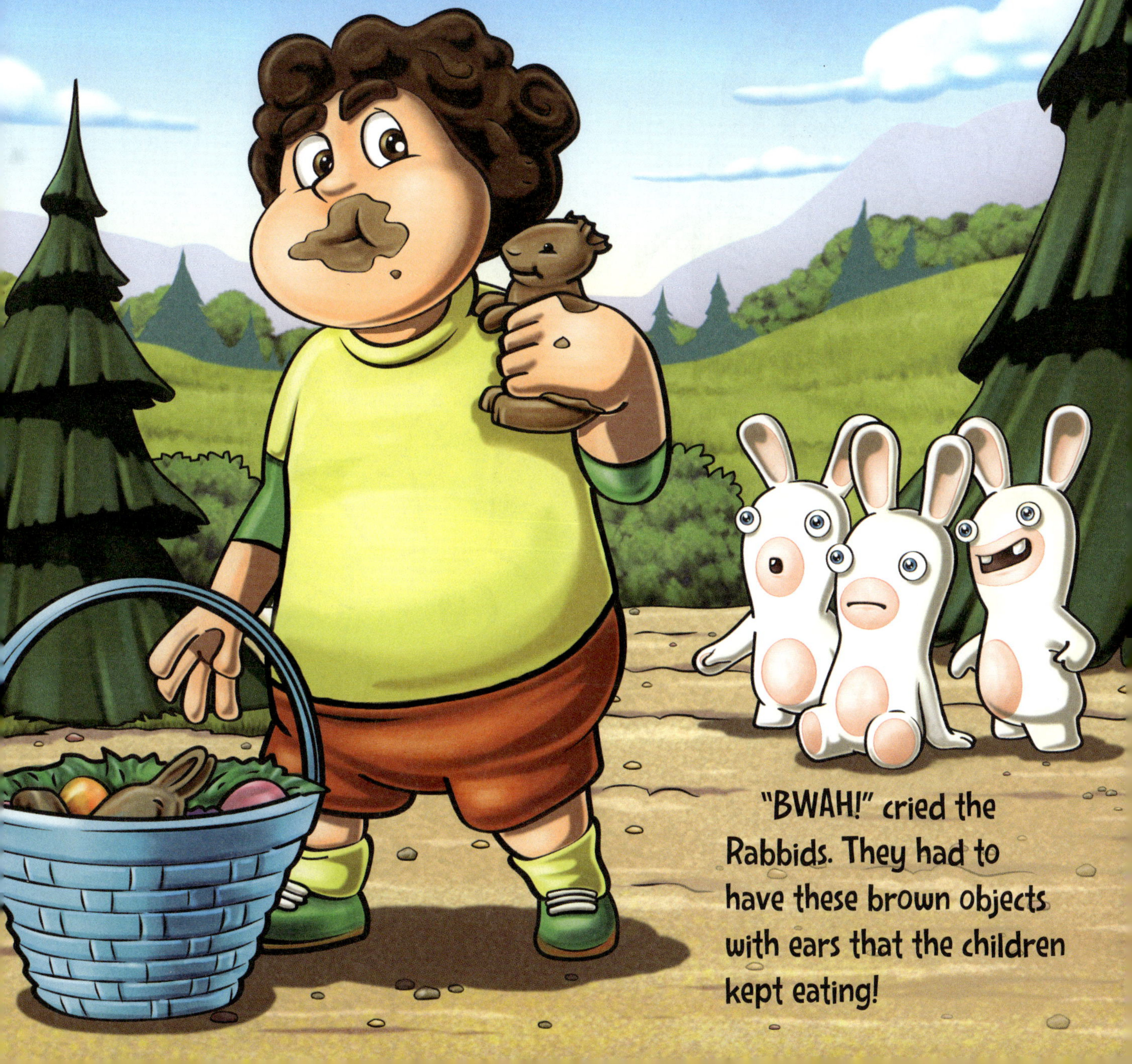

"BWAH!" cried the Rabbids. They had to have these brown objects with ears that the children kept eating!

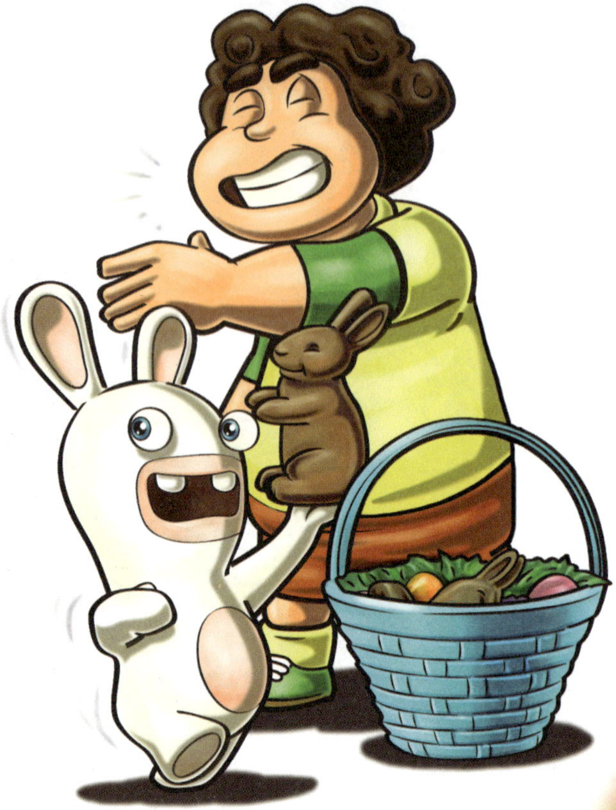

So they abandoned the parade and went around taking candy from children . . .

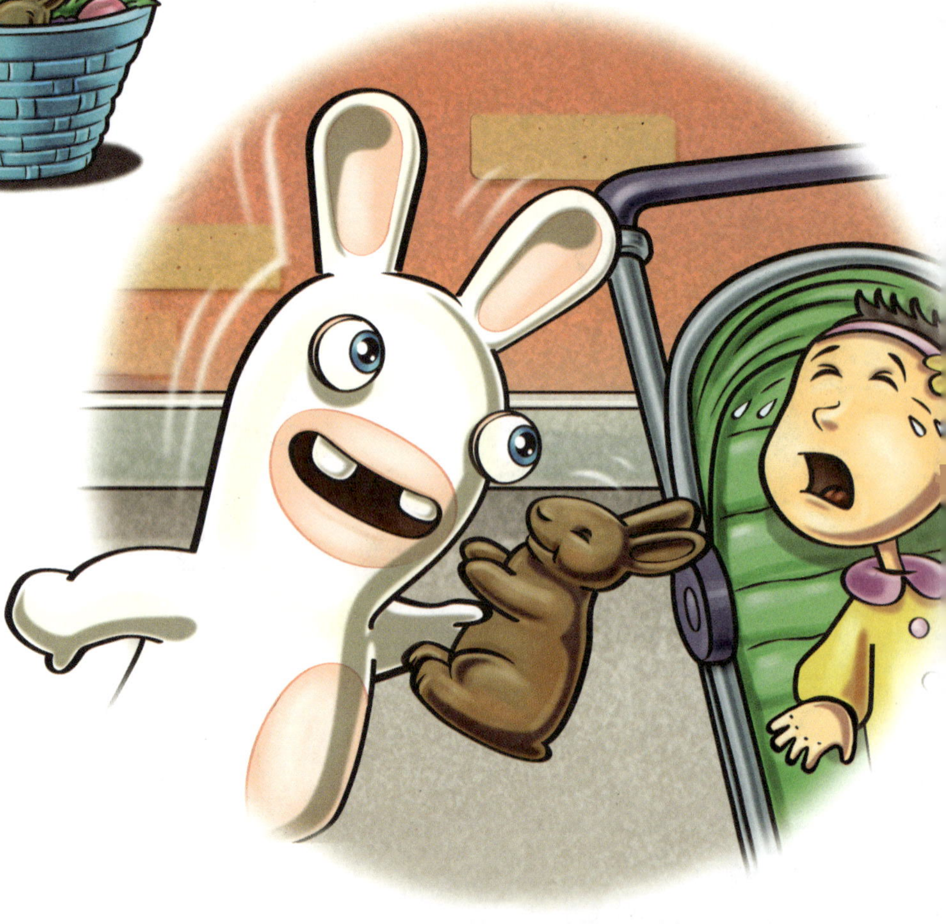

and babies . . .

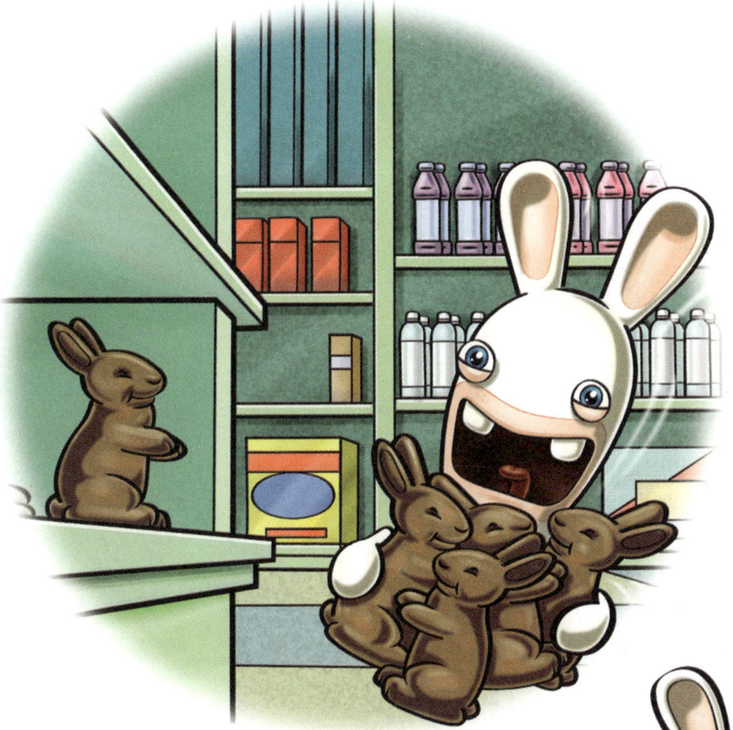

and stores.

Oh, my!

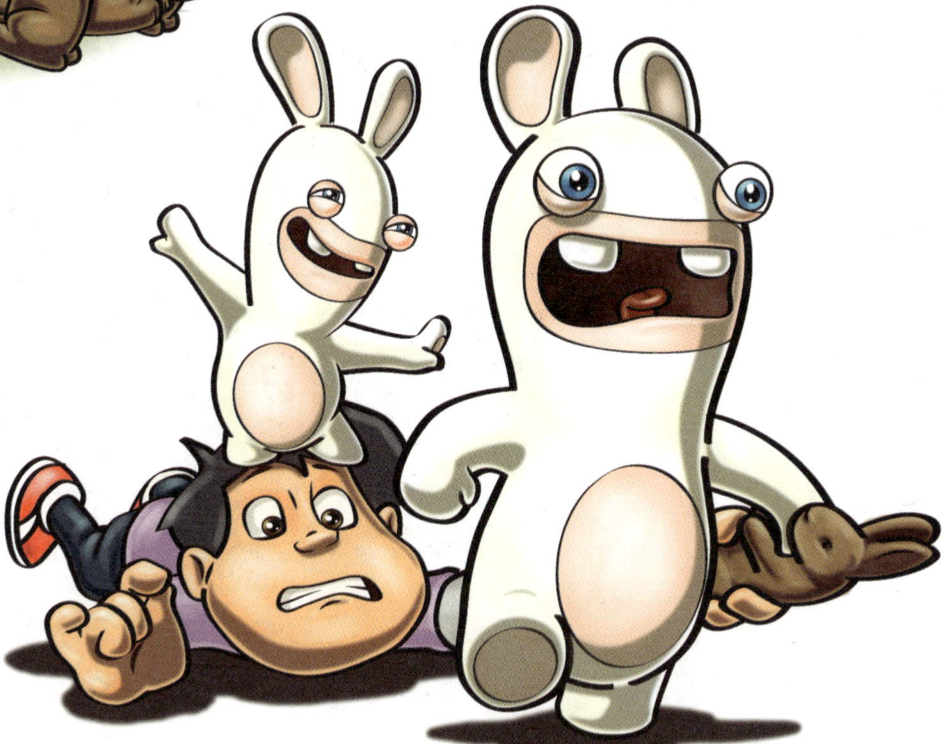

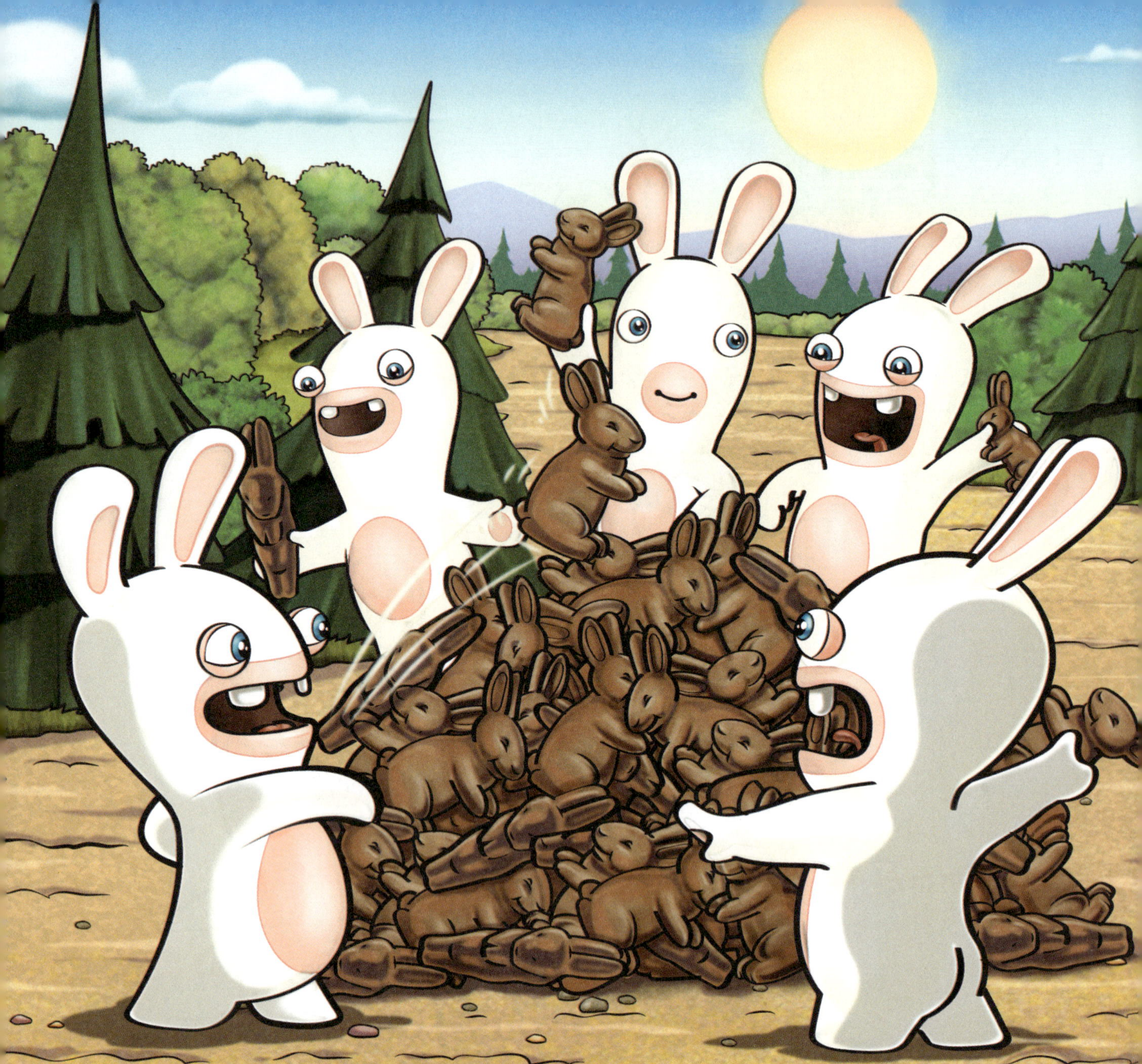

It wasn't long before the Rabbids had their hands on a lot of chocolate bunnies.

At that point the kids had had it. The Rabbids had ruined their Easter egg hunt, turned their Easter parade into a disaster, and taken away the absolute best part of Easter: their candy!

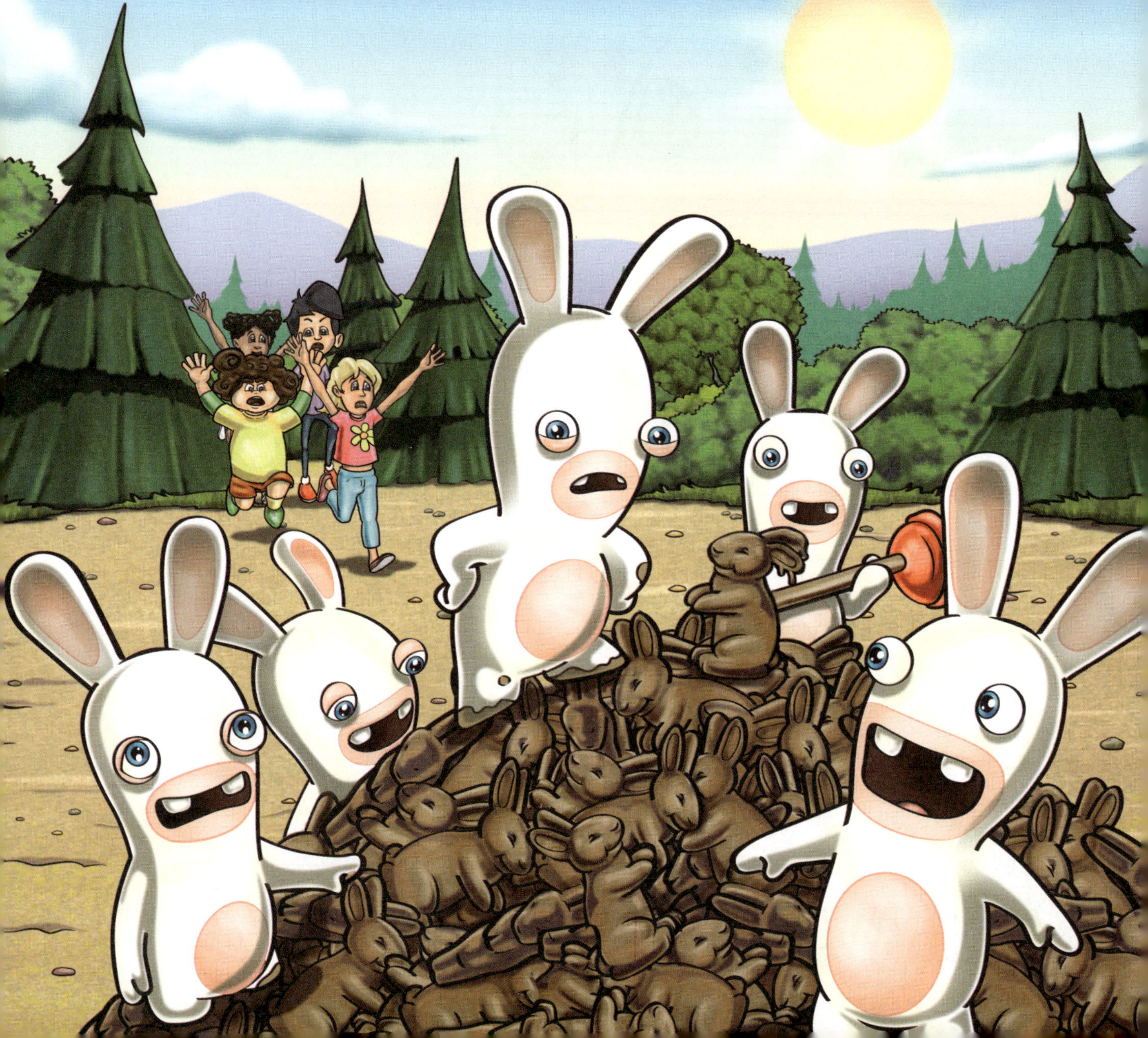

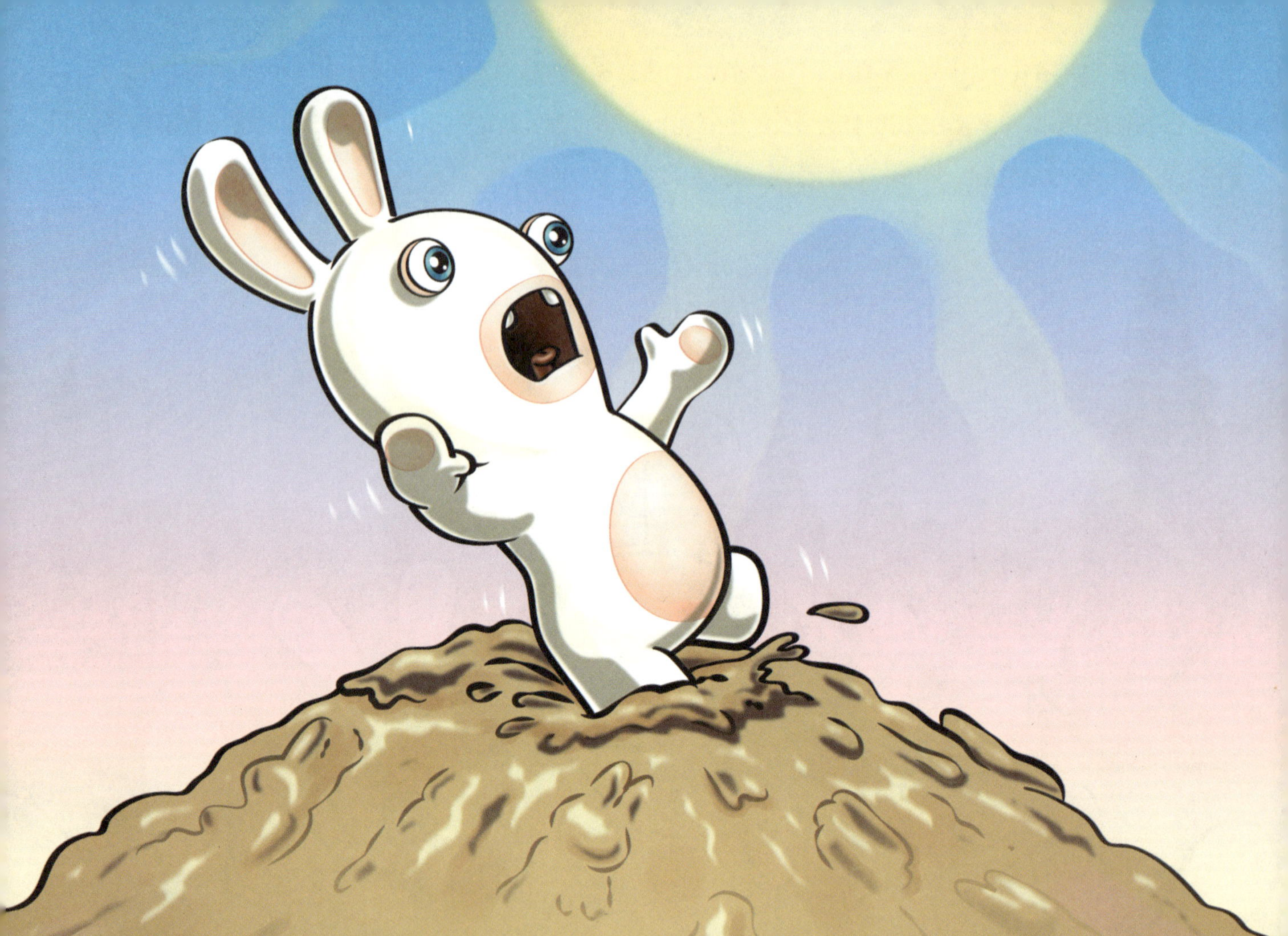

The swarm of kids started to approach the chocolate mountain.

"Bwah, bwah bwah bwah BWAH," shouted the Rabbid on the top of the mountain, ordering the children to stop. But it was hard for him to look commanding, because he was having trouble staying on his feet. These brown bunnies were turning . . . mushy!

"BWAAAAAAH!" cried the Rabbid as he lost his balance and went sliding rapidly down the melting chocolate mountain.

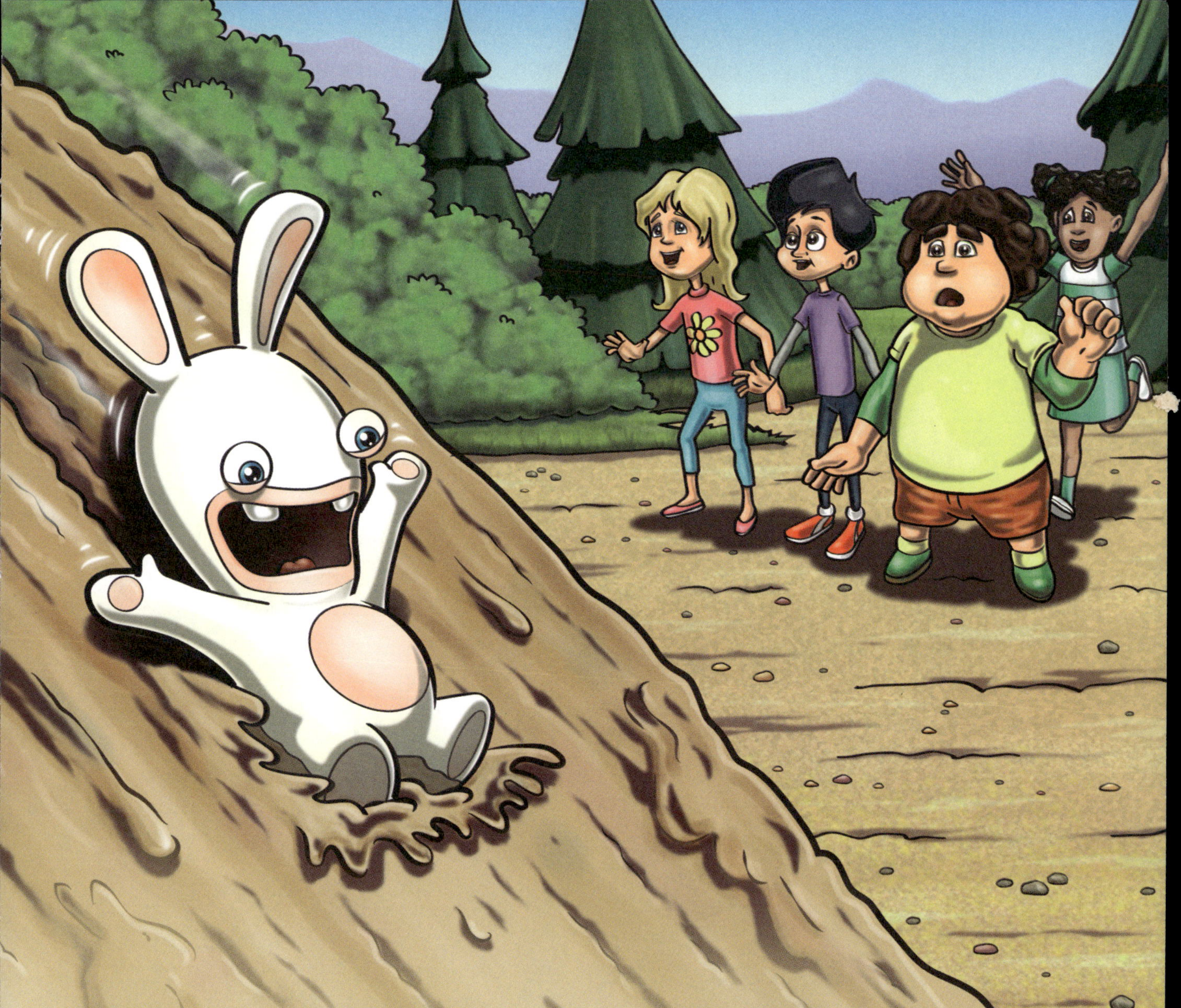

The kids stopped marching and stared in awe at the Rabbid who had just slid down the chocolate bunny mountain and now had chocolate all over his butt. Then they all raced to take their turn on the giant chocolate slide!

It's unlikely that the Rabbids will remember what happened on Easter, but for the kids . . . it was the best Easter ever.

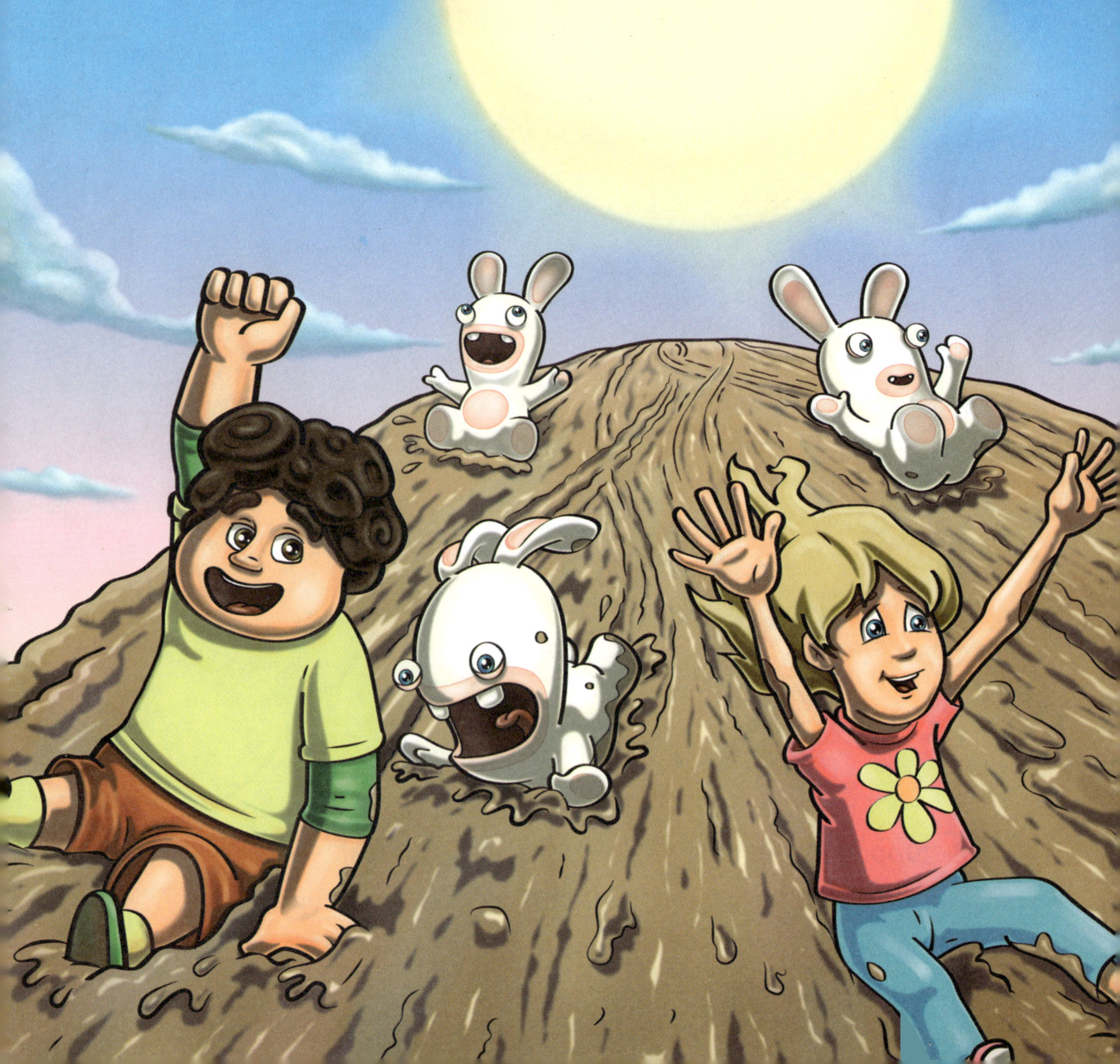